a greyhound
A GROUNDHOG

written by

EMILY JENKINS

illustrated by

CHRIS APPELHANS

schwartz & wade books · new york

A Greyhound, a Groundhog
owes a debt
of inspiration
and rhythm
to
A Very Special House,
by legendary children's author
Ruth Krauss.
It's for her,
though I never met her,
as a thanks.
—E.J.

For Oliver
—C.A.

Text copyright © 2017 by Emily Jenkins • Jacket art and interior illustrations copyright © 2017 by Chris Appelhans • All rights reserved. Published in the United States by Schwartz & Wade Books, an imprint of Random House Children's Books, a division of Penguin Random House LLC, New York. • Schwartz & Wade Books and the colophon are trademarks of Penguin Random House LLC. • Visit us on the Web! randomhousekids.com • Educators and librarians, for a variety of teaching tools, visit us at RHTeachersLibrarians.com • *Library of Congress Cataloging-in-Publication Data* Names: Jenkins, Emily, author. | Appelhans, Chris, illustrator. Title: A greyhound, a groundhog / Emily Jenkins; illustrated by Chris Appelhans. Description: First edition. | New York: Schwartz & Wade, 2017. | Summary: A tongue twister featuring a little round greyhound and a little round groundhog who work themselves into a frenzy as they whirl around and around one another. Identifiers: LCCN 2016000753 (print) | LCCN 2016025454 (ebook) | ISBN 978-0-553-49805-9 (hardback) | ISBN 978-0-553-49806-6 (glb) | ISBN 978-0-553-49807-3 (ebook) Subjects: | CYAC: Stories in rhyme. | Greyhounds—Fiction. | Dogs—Fiction. | Woodchuck—Fiction. | Tongue twisters. | BISAC: JUVENILE FICTION / Concepts / Words. | JUVENILE FICTION / Concepts / Size & Shape. | JUVENILE FICTION / Animals / Dogs. Classification: LCC PZ8.3.J3983 Gr 2017 (print) | LCC PZ8.3.J3983 (ebook) | DDC [E]—dc23

The text of this book is set in Belen.
The illustrations were rendered in watercolor and pencil.

MANUFACTURED IN CHINA
10 9 8 7 6 5 4 3 2 1
First Edition

A hound.

A round hound.

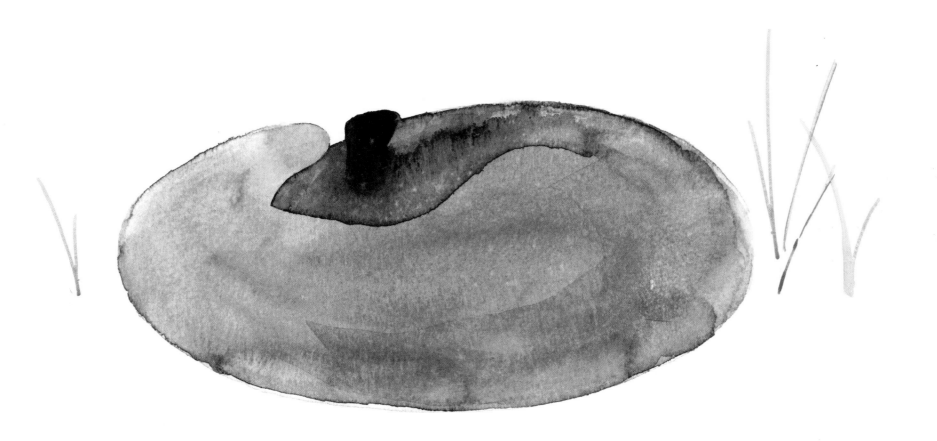

A greyhound.

A hog.

A round hog.

A groundhog.

A groundhog, a greyhound,

a round little

greyhound.

A greyhound, a groundhog,

a brown little

groundhog.

A groundhog, a greyhound,

a grey little

round hound.

A greyhound, a groundhog,
a found little
roundhog.

Around, round hound.

Around, groundhog!

Around, brown hog.

Around, grey dog!

Around and

around and around

and around.

The ground and a hog and some grey and a dog.

a grey dog,

A round hound,

a round little hound dog.

A greyhog,

a ground dog,

a hog little hound dog.

Around and around

and astound

and astound!

A bog

and a sound

and a log on the ground

and around and around and around

and around!